CREEPERS

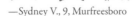

The Scarecrow

by Edgar J. Hyde

Illustrations by Chloe Tyler

PAB-0608-0302 • ISBN: 978-1-4867-1878-8

Copyright ©2020 Flowerpot Press, a Division of Flowerpot Children's Press, Inc., Oakville, ON, Canada.

Printed and bound in the U.S.A.

Table of Contents

CHAPTER ONE

A New Day

"David, hurry up! Your breakfast is almost ready."

David Davies rolled over in bed and groaned. School again. He loved that twilight zone between deep sleep and getting out of bed. He had been thinking about last weekend. His dad had taken him to the baseball game for the first time in years. It was the playoffs, and the Rockets won! What a game! A huge crowd, countless great plays, and…

"David, get a move on!" his mom screamed at the top of her lungs.

"I'm coming, I'm coming," David moaned, his mom's shrill voice disturbing his peace.

David jumped out of bed, went to the bathroom, and quickly got dressed. He looked around his room for the shoes he'd worn the night before. His room was covered in the usual adolescent mess of clothing, sports gear, and video games.

After a few minutes, he appeared in the downstairs hallway, dressed in what could loosely be described as the school uniform. Well, he had the school tie on at least. The rest was questionable at best. Baggy shirt, baggy sweater, and baggy pants.

David's two sisters were already halfway through their bowls of cornflakes or oatmeal or whatever healthy concoction they were into these days. In David's opinion, having two older sisters was the worst bad joke God could have played on a boy. David had just turned thirteen, Sarah was fourteen (and a half, as she liked to remind everyone) and Emma was almost sixteen.

Between their fascination with clothes and makeup, David felt, at times, that life was almost unbearable.

"David, the school bus is going to be here in fifteen minutes and look at you!" his mom said with a sigh.

"Okay, Mom, relax. Where's Dad?" David asked, peering out of the kitchen window.

"He is over in the far field checking on some of the sheep. He thinks that fox has been back again. The chickens were making an awful racket last night. He'll be back in a minute," replied Mrs. Davies, throwing some toast onto David's plate.

David's dad was a farmer and the family had just recently moved to the area. The new farm was massive and at least three times the size of the farm they had lived on before. Not only did they have more sheep and cattle, but they had far more land to manage.

The only problem was that David's dad had

so much work to do that he had very little time to spend with his son. With only two sisters for company on an isolated farm, David could be a handful at times. Boredom easily set in, and he was always getting into trouble for his antics. His imagination and his bad taste in practical jokes were always the cause of friction between he and his sisters. He could tolerate Sarah, but he had no time at all for Emma. He thought she was from another planet.

"Emma, meeting Steve at lunchtime again today?" David asked, smirking at his oldest sister.

"Mom, tell him to mind his own business. I refuse to talk to him after Friday's performance. He is so embarrassing." Emma pouted, turning away.

Emma was referring to the teasing or, more accurately, abuse David and his friends had subjected Emma and her "boyfriend" to when he had spotted them walking hand in hand on the way to class. Steve was a fair target in David's mind—although he had been forced to make a quick escape when the almost six-foot Steve had decided he had had enough and went after his new love's younger brother.

"Emma, don't give me any grief," David whispered, "or I'll tell them what I saw you doing on Wednesday, and how that didn't look like Steve to me, even though it was hard to tell for sure with you all over him!"

"You're a jerk!" Emma snapped, storming off to her room.

Sarah followed Emma, scowling at her brother, as only sisters know how to.

"David, give it a rest. I'm fed up with all this bickering!" barked Mrs. Davies. "Eat your breakfast."

David looked out the window again. His dad had just climbed over the fence next to the large barn where they stored most of the winter hay. The barn was also home to the family's hens. He was carrying the double-barreled shotgun he usually took out to scare off unwanted visitors. Foxes and crows were the usual targets. David opened the kitchen door and ran out to meet his dad.

"Hey Dad, everything alright?" David asked. "Any problem with the sheep?"

"Nope, everything seems okay," Mr. Davies replied. "That fox must have left. Those chickens woke me up again last night. What a noise! Just wait until we get ourselves a new dog next week. That'll scare him off!"

David's old family dog had disappeared two weeks ago. Nobody knew what had happened to him. David's dad had guessed he had fallen down some old foxhole and not been able to get out. He had been a good dog for making sure the local foxes were kept at bay. But now he was gone. It had upset David. The dog was often David's only companion on the farm, and they had spent a lot of time together.

"Do me a favor, Davy, will you?" Mr. Davies shouted as he kicked off his boots outside the kitchen door. "Go and get me half a dozen eggs from the barn. I could do with a couple of nice fresh boiled eggs. I'm starving."

"Sure, Dad," David replied, running off to the barn, happy to help his dad.

"Morning, where's my coffee?" Mr. Davies demanded jokingly as he opened the kitchen door.

"Where it usually is, in the pot. Help yourself," Mrs. Davies replied, cleaning up the girls' dishes. "I hope you took off those dirty boots."

They were both stopped in their tracks with a sudden, chilling scream from the barn.

"Daad, Daad! Help! Help!"

"Get out there, John, that's David!"

CHAPTER TWO

Stranger

Mr. Davies burst out of the kitchen door and crossed the yard as fast as he could. He ran into the barn, his eyes darting all over, searching for his son. Besides the light from the barn entrance, the barn was completely dark. The early morning sunshine had not yet penetrated the barn's broad span.

"David, where are you? Are you all right?" Mr. Davies stammered, his eyes trying to peer through the darkness as they adjusted from the bright sunshine.

"Daad, Daaaaad!"

The farmer caught sight of his son standing in the far corner of the barn. He rushed to his side.

"David, are you okay? What's going on?" Mr. Davies asked worriedly.

David appeared to be uninjured. He was standing straight, his mouth open with his lower jaw almost on his chest. His eyes were glazed over and fixed straight ahead. David's dad scanned his son from head to toe, running his hands up and down his son's body.

"What happened to you? Did you fall? Are you hurt?" his dad asked, his voice becoming less frantic as he could see no obvious injury.

But David still stared ahead, his eyes fixed as if in shock. Eventually, David turned his gaze toward his dad's face. His dad looked into his son's eyes and followed his gaze as David once again turned his head to look straight ahead. At the same time, David raised his arm, his finger pointed toward a figure about four feet from where they stood.

There was no need for David to point now. His dad could see what was holding his son's stare.

Four feet away, lying on a pile of hay, was a dark shape. At first the shape was difficult to make out. However, it quickly became unmistakable. It was a body. A man's body.

Mr. Davies feared the worst. But the body was not still and the body's eyes were not closed. The man was alive! Mr. Davies could clearly see the body shaking all over, as if connected to some constant electrical charge, and the whites of two eyes sharply pierced the dimness of the barn.

"Go into the house, David. Tell your mom you're all right," Mr. Davies whispered, pushing David away with his broad hand and staring at the mysterious and unwelcome figure.

There was no need. David's mom had followed her husband across the yard, and the sound of her arrival at the barn entrance seemed to inject more electrical charge into the shaking figure and cause the already wide white eyes to open wider.

"Stay back, Karen. David, you too. Go see to

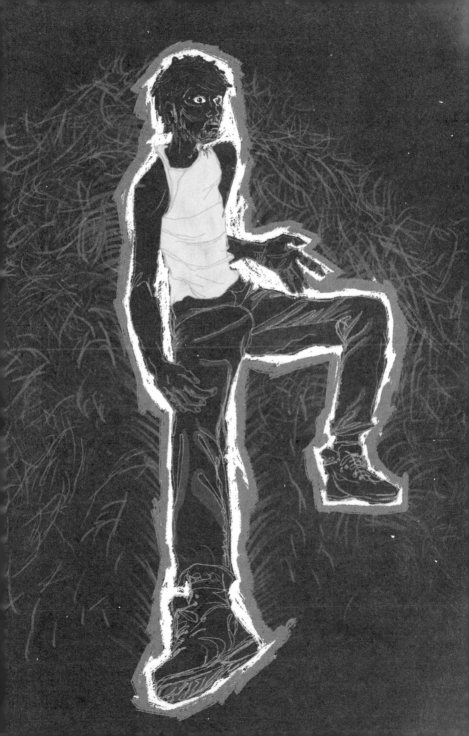

your mom, son."

But David was still too shocked to move. He watched as his father edged closer to the trembling figure. Mr. Davies reached out his hand and laid it firmly on the man's shoulder.

"Who in the world are you? What happened to you? What are you doing here?" Mr. Davies's voice trembled, betraying the nervousness they all felt.

His approach and contact only seemed to send another 200 volts into the already shock-ridden body. To everyone's surprise, the man jumped up and in one movement, threw the big farmer to the floor and headed for the barn entrance. David's dad was a big man, and it seemed unlikely that he could so easily be pushed down by a man who looked no more than half his size.

The sudden movement seemed to shake David from his trance. Seeing his dad thrown to the floor, David threw himself at the man's feet, sending him hurtling into the numerous chicken coops that housed the family's army of hens. Among the flapping wings and tangled chicken wire, the man struggled to get to his feet.

But there was no point. David's dad was now back on his feet and no longer in any mood to hold back on this unwelcome visitor. Any concern or sympathy he had previously felt was now gone. Mr. Davies's foot buried itself deep into the man's stomach. Once, twice, then a third time, followed swiftly by a right hook square to his jaw. The man slumped to the floor semi-conscious.

"David, go with your mom. Call the police. They'll have to attend to this now. I'll stay with him until they get here," Mr. Davies instructed, his voice now full of his usual composure.

David ran over to his mom and the two quickly made their way to the house, eager to call for help.

"Well then, stranger, what do you have to say for yourself?" Mr. Davies questioned, lifting the man to his feet and sitting him down on top of one of the overturned chicken coops.

The man's body had stopped shaking, but his eyes were as wide as ever, displaying what now in clearer light seemed like sheer terror.

"Come on, speak up," Mr. Davies insisted.

The man looked hard into Mr. Davies's eyes, his own eyes seeming to search the farmer's for help.

"Well? What are you doing here? Tell me!" Mr. Davies shouted, losing patience. He grabbed and shook the man's shoulder, frustrated by the lack of response.

The man opened his mouth, and a trickle of blood appeared at the corner of his lips. He seemed to mutter something, but it was no more than a garble and barely audible.

"What? What are you trying to say? Speak up! Speak up!" insisted Mr. Davies.

Again, the stranger started to open his mouth and again, no sense could be made of the noises he made. His two hands went to his mouth, as if trying to pry out the words he seemed unable to utter. The noises he was making were no more than moans and groans. He then crumbled to the floor with noises that, this time, were unmistakable. The man was sobbing uncontrollably. Mr. Davies looked down bemused at the pathetic figure in front of him.

"Well, you'll talk soon enough when you're behind bars. You better have something to say for yourself then," Mr. Davies snapped, offering no pity to the stranger.

CHAPTER THREE

Not a Stranger

Three days had passed since the episode in the barn. The police had seemed to take forever to show up. While they waited, Mr. Davies had been unable to get any information out of the strange visitor.

Once the police eventually did appear, the stranger was no longer a stranger. He was well known to the police. His name apparently was John Morrison. He was a local thief, somebody who was very familiar with the inside of a jail cell. He had a police record as long as his arm.

According to the police, he had been a real tough guy in his time, and the sight of him broken down and sobbing, the way he had been that day, had really puzzled them. Morrison was not easily intimidated or frightened by anyone.

He had still not said an intelligible word up to the time he was thrown, wailing, into the back of the police car.

David was in his room, still a little preoccupied by the recent experience, wondering about it all, when he heard the doorbell ring. He hadn't seen or heard the police car approach as he was lost in his own world, imagining all the possible causes that had brought that strange man to their barn in that state.

"David! Will you get that? My hands are covered at the moment," Mrs. Davies shouted from outside the kitchen backdoor.

David's mom had been cleaning up the mess in the chicken coops. So who knows what her hands were covered in.

David ran down the stairs. The shape through

the glass of the front door was unmistakable. It was a police officer.

David opened the door.

"Good morning, son. Is your dad in?" Officer Collins asked, looking past David into the hallway.

It took about fifteen minutes for David to retrieve his dad from his tractor in one of the fields close by. He was still angry with the intruder who had upset his family, and he wanted no more to do with it. The police officer's visit only disturbed his busy day.

In the meantime, David's mom, hands suitably cleaned, had given the patient officer some cookies and coffee. Throughout the fifteen-minute wait, he had remained straight-faced and unwilling to give any hint as to the purpose of his visit.

Eventually everyone had gathered in the front room. Emma and Sarah had come down from their rooms. There was no way that they were going to miss the excitement. It wasn't every day that their house was the center of police activity. Although Emma seemed more interested in admiring the officer's blue eyes and how they matched his blue uniform. David just looked at his sisters and shook his head in mock disgust.

Officer Collins stood up and walked to the window. He seemed a little reluctant to talk. After a few seconds, he turned around and said, "I am afraid I have some upsetting news." He paused. "Maybe you would prefer that the children leave the room, Mr. Davies?" the officer suggested, looking first at David and then the girls.

"No, it's fine, officer. Go ahead. They are all old enough now," he replied.

"All right, sir. I am sorry to tell you that the man we apprehended here the other day, Mr. John Morrison, is now in a coma."

The officer hesitated. He looked at the faces around the room. It wasn't as if they'd known the man well, but the officer's words stunned them. It was a mixture of shock and confusion. The image of the man trembling in the barn and then being escorted away by the police was still fresh in all their minds.

"What happened?" Mr. Davies asked tentatively.

The officer continued, "After we left here the other day, Morrison was taken to the police station. The whole way, it was impossible to make any sense of what he was trying to say. I had met Morrison before, two or three times, and he was a smart guy. A criminal, yes, but sharp and witty. He was always full of jokes. I couldn't believe this was the same man in the car with us that night. It was clear something significant had happened to him. His inability to speak sensibly mixed with the fear and pain we could see on his face disturbed us."

David looked around the room. His sisters' silly grins had disappeared and his mother's face looked ashen. His dad's face was expressionless.

"As soon as we booked him into the station, we called in the doctor on duty. He was only in the man's cell a minute or two when he called us in to ask who the man was and if any of us had spoken to him recently. I confirmed that I knew him and had spoken to him several times in the past.

"I told him it had been about a month since we had arrested him last on suspicion of robbery and that he was very vocal then. We couldn't shut him up! He complained constantly of being harassed.

"The doctor said that he may never talk again. He informed us that Morrison had no tongue. It was just gone from his mouth."

At this the police officer stopped. He obviously was still affected by the details of his story.

The room was silent now, and the faces and expressions were becoming even more confused.

"Goodness, what happened? His tongue? But how?" Mr. Davies asked, his voice was a mixture of shock and amazement.

"Please wait, sir, let me continue," the officer interrupted.

"All of us at the station were stunned too. But the concern for Morrison didn't stop there. The man was ranting and raving like a lunatic, unable to speak, but making plenty of noise. He was jumping around, his eyes staring like a mad dog. He was in real danger of injuring himself. The doctor quickly insisted that he be taken to the hospital where he could be properly evaluated. So he was transferred immediately. I accompanied him myself in the transfer, and I was there when they signed him in. They had just given him a strong sedative and thankfully, at last, he was beginning to calm down. I was feeling very relieved to be able to go home. Morrison's injuries and behavior were really disturbing. I had never seen anything like it.

"The next morning, I got to the station at my usual time. But as soon as I entered the office, I could tell that something was wrong. There was a real atmosphere about the place. I had just reached my desk when Captain Grant called me into his office.

"'Collins,' he said, his face as stern as I had ever seen it. 'Morrison's in a coma. He simply faded out some time during the night. The doctor was just here. He's already been moved up to the hospital and they say he's showing almost no signs of life. Strange business. What on earth happened?'

"I couldn't believe what I was hearing. The whole episode was becoming more and more unbelievable. I couldn't understand what could possibly have caused Morrison that type of injury and left him in that condition.

"The captain wasn't finished though. A crumpled piece of paper was sitting in the middle of his desk, and he pushed it toward me. 'Take a look at this,' he said. 'They found it in Morrison's bed. It looks like his writing.'"

At that, the officer stopped and put his hand into his jacket pocket and pulled out a crumpled piece of paper.

"This is the note. It's completely ridiculous, but the captain asked me to show it to you and see if it would mean anything to you, seeing as he was found on your property."

The officer leaned over and passed the paper to Mr. Davies. David and the two girls all ran behind his chair. Only Mrs. Davies remained where she was. Mr. Davies smoothed out the paper and held it out in front of him. The writing was messy, but the words were clear enough.

God help me. God help us all. I beg you to believe me. I am so scared, but I am not crazy. I have never been so scared in all my life. I can't stand it. I was attacked by a wooden monster, a monster that came to life in front of my very eyes. He will find me here. He will come for me. I begged him to spare me. I was only going to take a few things—a radio, some money—no big deal. But this wooden monster, this scarecrow, would not let me go. You must stop him! Stop him! I beg you!

Mr. Davies stood up, thrusting the note back into the police officer's hand.

"What is this nonsense? The man was obviously crazy. Wooden monster? Scarecrow? This whole thing is just ridiculous."

The officer moved toward the living room door.

"So I take it this all means nothing to you too?" he asked. "We had to check, just in case."

"Of course it doesn't make any sense," Mr. Davies snapped angrily. "This man came onto our land, upset my family, and now he's spun this story? This is the last I want to hear of all this."

"Well, thank you, anyway," Officer Collins said, heading to the hallway. "I am sorry to have disturbed you. The whole episode is disturbing for us all. We don't get much of this sort of thing here."

Officer Collins went out to his car and drove off. Mr. Davies walked out of the house, shaking his head, toward the field where he left his tractor. Mrs. Davies went to the kitchen and made some coffee. She needed a cup. The two girls ran upstairs, upset by the story they had just heard.

Only David remained in the room. He sat motionless, staring out the living room window. His eyes seemed fixed on something. If you had followed his gaze, you would have seen the distant figure in the far field. The old farm scarecrow.

CHAPTER FOUR

Gotta Know More

David stared out the window. He couldn't take his eyes off the scarecrow looming out there. The scarecrow stood in an uncultivated field next to the house. It was a field that his father still hadn't had time to work on. It had always seemed strange to David that the only scarecrow on the farm stood in a field that didn't need one. His dad had continually said that he was going to move it. But like many other jobs on the farm, it just hadn't been done.

David was confused, and he was becoming a little scared. As he stared at the erect figure in the field, he began to think of his old dog. He had been satisfied with his dad's version of the dog's disappearance. After all, the old dog had been constantly chasing foxes and getting stuck down foxholes was a regular demise for overzealous hounds. However, he had never mentioned to anyone, especially his dad, the other version that had been suggested for the dog's absence.

Two days after the dog had gone missing, David had been standing on the road outside the farm, waiting for the school bus. He was upset. His dog had never disappeared before. His dad had told him that he would probably never see his old friend again. His sisters, as usual, were late and hadn't come out yet. An old man had appeared suddenly at his side, the smell of alcohol announcing his arrival as much as anything. He had been sleeping under a nearby hedge. Old Jonesy was a well-known local celebrity. He was a down-and-out drunk, rarely sober enough to recognize whether it was night or day. However, he could often bring a smile to your face with his quick wit and his many stories.

"Ah, young Davy, how are you? What's wrong? Why so glum?" Jonesy had asked, noticing the boy's concerned face.

"We haven't seen Sandy, our dog, since yesterday evening. He's disappeared," David had replied.

Jonesy's grin left his face and was replaced with a deep frown.

"Well, son, you'll never see him again. He's gone for sure. Gone forever," the old man mumbled.

"Gone? What do you mean?" David had pressed, a little agitated.

The old man put his arm around David. The smell of stale alcohol was overpowering.

He continued, "He ran off. I saw him with my own eyes. Chased off by that wooden thing, that scarecrow over there!"

The old man jerked his head in the direction of the farm and continued, "That thing chased him all the way over the fields. The animal was howling like a banshee. No, you won't see him again."

David had laughed at the time. The thought of the scarecrow running across his dad's fields chasing after his old dog was the sort of crazy story Old Jonesy was famous for.

But as David recalled the encounter with the old man now, he was not laughing. In fact, he was beginning to feel more and more scared. Morrison's note had talked about a wooden monster—a scarecrow. Was it a coincidence? Just nonsense spoken by two madmen? He couldn't tell his dad about Old Jonesy's story. He would just laugh at him. But now, after reading Morrison's note, it was all becoming a little weird.

David decided he had to find Old Jonesy again. He had to talk to him about what the old man had seen that night. As he headed out the door, David glanced out the window and peered at the wooden shape in the field and shook his head.

David ran to the shed beside the house, pulled out his bike, and rode off as fast as he could toward town.

It usually took David about twenty minutes to ride into town, but this time the journey seemed like less than half of that. Jonesy had a number of usual hangouts in town during the day. He would normally be trying to make some money or be spending money on his staple diet of cheap wine.

It didn't take David long to catch sight of him. He was propped up at the corner of one of the town's two bars, held upright by a combination of the side of the building and a large overflowing trash can.

David quickly rode over and shouted to the old man. The old man didn't respond. David climbed off his bike and walked slowly to the corner of the bar. Still, the old man's head was down and slumped on his chest.

"Jonesy, it's me, Davy. I have to talk to you," David said, approaching the old man.

"Jonesy, are you okay? It's me, Davy," he added, becoming a little agitated by the old man's lack of response.

Finally, the old man raised his head. David was instantly shocked. Jonesy looked into his eyes. David immediately recognized the look in the old man's eyes. It was that same frightened stare that he had seen on Morrison's face in the barn. David hesitated, almost too scared to speak.

"Jonesy, what happened? Are you okay?" David asked, taking the old man's arm.

The old man started to shake his head, and David spotted tears welling up in his eyes. The old man started to open his mouth. David spotted, for the first time, the dried blood clinging to the old man's beard. As he opened his mouth wider, David gasped and staggered back.

Jonesy's tongue was gone.

CHAPTER FIVE

A Regular Farm Scarecrow

If the trip to town had been fast, the trip back was even faster. When he had made it home, David had thrown his bike into the shed and sprinted through the house, up the stairs, and into his room, slamming the door hard behind him.

His mind was totally jumbled, a mixture of confusion and fear. But what could he do? Who could he talk to? He was pretty convinced now that there was real danger close by. Two men connected with his house had both lost their tongues, and his dog's disappearance seemed somehow connected. Even if it had nothing to do with a scarecrow coming to life, there was something going on that had frightened these two men, leaving both speechless and one in a coma.

David sat through dinner in silence, barely touching his food. His mind preoccupied with the scarecrow. He still hadn't said anything to anyone.

"Well at least we can all sleep in tomorrow," said Mrs. Davies.

"Thank God for that! That rooster was beginning to drive me crazy," added Mr. Davies.

David looked up, not quite understanding the significance of the conversation.

"Well someone better go and get rid of it before it starts smelling up the place," Mrs. Davies insisted.

"Honey, this is a farm. One more bad smell is hardly going to make a difference," Mr. Davies replied with a broad grin on his face. "I'll figure it out later," he added quickly, seeing the scowl appearing on his wife's face.

David started to pay attention.

"What are you talking about?" he asked. "What's going on?"

Sarah chimed in, "David, where has your head been all day? Sometimes you don't have a clue!"

"Your dad found the rooster dead beside the barn this morning. The poor thing must have just been too old, probably fell off the top of the barn. Either that or your dad threw his boot at it at half-past five this morning," Mrs. Davies explained.

"Where is it now?" David asked, standing up.

"Same place. Don't worry, I'll figure it out after dinner," Mr. Davies said, seeing concern in his son's face.

But it was more than concern on David's face. David knew he had to see the bird. He had to check something out. After dinner, he immediately ran out of the kitchen and across the yard to the barn.

"What's gotten into him all of a sudden?" Mr.

Davies asked. "He hated the noise the darn thing made every morning too."

David turned the corner of the barn and immediately saw the dead bird on top of an old farm fence. David looked up to the top of the barn. The bird was positioned directly under the spot on the roof where he could be found every morning at sunrise. Well, where he used to be found.

Maybe Mom was right, David thought. The rooster probably fell off the roof.

But the more David thought about it, the more he knew it didn't sound right. Birds don't fall off roofs. David looked to his left and less than twenty yards away stood the figure that was becoming more and more sinister—the scarecrow.

There it stood, harmless looking enough, but intimidating all the same. David looked again at the dead rooster lying in front of him. David stepped forward and leaned down. He picked up a stick and prodded the bird. It was dead all right. The rooster's head was hidden underneath its body. David used the stick to pry the head out. He flicked the stick and the whole bird rolled over.

The rooster's head was visible now. The head and neck were limp, the way David had seen many times when his dad had decided it was going to be chicken for Sunday dinner. His dad had shown David how to kill a chicken by wringing its neck and had even suggested he try it. David had always declined. He thought it looked so cruel.

This rooster looked as if it had died the same way. Its head and neck were contorted and twisted. There was only one more thing to do. David had to look inside the bird's mouth. He had to know if this incident could be tied to all the other events.

David dropped the stick and kneeled on the ground. With one hand, he grabbed the bird by the neck and lifted it up. With his other hand, he pried open its beak. David knew exactly what to expect this time. There was no shock, but there was fear. The rooster's tiny tongue was gone.

"David, what on earth are you doing? Put that thing down," Mr. Davies shouted as he turned the corner.

David was still kneeling on the ground and holding the bird by the neck. When he heard his dad, he threw it to the ground.

"What has gotten into you, David? That thing is putrid," added Mr. Davies.

David stood up, frightened and confused. Mr. Davies could see there was something wrong.

"What is it, David? You look like you've seen a ghost. It was only an old rooster. The thing was a darn nuisance. I'm almost glad he passed," Mr. Davies said, picking the bird up and throwing it into a garbage bag he had brought from the kitchen.

David couldn't get any words out. He wanted to tell his dad that this was the third time, today alone, he had seen or heard about somebody or something losing its tongue. But Mr. Davies had already dismissed Morrison's note as the work of a madman. He certainly wouldn't take Old Jonesy seriously, and a dead rooster was not going to convince him of much either. David couldn't say anything yet.

But he was so scared, he had to do something. He felt there was real danger on the farm.

Mr. Davies disappeared around the back of the barn, where most of the farm waste was dumped, carrying the dead rooster. David looked again at the wooden figure in the field. He was really frightened now, but he had to do it. He had to take a close look at the scarecrow.

David waited by the barn until he heard the noise of his dad returning to the kitchen. It was beginning to get dark now, and the kitchen lights were beginning to spread across the duskiness of the yard. Once David heard the kitchen door close, he approached the wooden fence separating the yard from the overgrown field. He looked back toward the kitchen. He could clearly see his mom in the kitchen cleaning up and his dad sitting at the table. Somehow, David felt a little bit less frightened and more secure knowing they were close by.

He climbed over the fence. The grass and weeds in the field stretched up to David's knees. As David struggled to put one foot in front of the other, he wondered again why his dad still hadn't worked on this field. His mom had certainly nagged him enough about it. She had continually said that she was fed up looking out of her kitchen window at the overgrown land in front of her.

David looked up. The darkening figure was now only a few yards away. David inhaled deeply, as if trying to hold his breath as he approached.

Finally, he was there. David let out a long gasp of air, almost in relief, trying to calm his nerves.

He didn't know what he had expected to see, but as he scanned the wooden man in front of him, he could see nothing, for the moment, that was out of the ordinary.

David was no expert on scarecrows, but this one looked like all the others he had seen on farms before. It looked like a regular farm scarecrow. Wooden head, broom handle arms, old suit, hat, and plenty of straw. Lots of straw. In fact, for such an old scarecrow that nobody had paid any attention to or looked after, it was in remarkably good shape. It didn't look years old, as it had to have been. The old lady that sold them the farm had briefly mentioned the scarecrow, saying that it had been there when she bought the farm twenty years earlier.

David was beginning to feel better. The incidents of the last few days were beginning to disappear in his mind as he looked at this unremarkable figure in front of him. David reached out to straighten the scarecrow's hat. He must have been a little nervous still, as his fingers twitched and the hat went tumbling to the ground. David leaned down and picked up the hat. He was just about to put it on top of the scarecrow's bald wooden head when he noticed that there was some writing engraved into the top of the scarecrow's head. David stood on his toes as he tried to make out the writing, but he struggled to get high enough to read the words clearly.

He looked around. It was getting very dark now. He could just make out the outline of a small pile of bricks a couple of yards away. David hurriedly lifted two or three bricks to the side of the scarecrow, putting one on top of the other. He stood up on the top brick. Standing a little shakily and holding the stretched out arm of the scarecrow, David could now see the words. David read silently and slowly to himself.

THIS LAND IS YOURS FOR YOU TO SCARE

ALL BEINGS WHO PERCHANCE DO DARE

TO DISTURB OR THREATEN WITHOUT PITY

THIS HOUSE'S PEACE AND PROSPERITY

This land is yours for you to scare
All beings who perchance do dare
To disturb or threaten without pity
This house's peace and prosperity.

David's feet slipped from the top brick and he fell to the ground. He got up and immediately ran to the fence and leapt over it in one movement. He ran as fast as his feet would carry him toward the safety of the kitchen light.

CHAPTER SIX

Believe Me!

David's sister Sarah sat alone in the kitchen. The rest of the family had moved to the living room. David had to say something to somebody now. He could no longer keep all that he knew and had seen to himself, but he was still too afraid to talk to his dad.

As David burst through the kitchen door, Sarah didn't even look up from her magazine. She was used to her brother scampering all over the house, running here and there in a constant hurry. David was a walking noise machine.

"Sarah," David started, his voice lowered in an attempt to ensure no one in the next room heard what he was about to say.

Sarah didn't lift her eyes from her magazine but answered, "What?"

"Sarah, listen to me. I have something really important to tell you," David continued.

Sarah looked at her brother now. She had sensed something different in her brother's voice. As she looked at him, she could see the worry on his face.

"What is it, David? You look terrible. Where have you been? I hope you haven't been messing with that dead rooster," Sarah said, wondering what was bothering her brother.

"Sarah, listen to me. I am going to tell you something kind of unbelievable. You have to trust me though. I need to tell someone before I lose my mind."

David related all the recent events. Sarah obviously knew the details about Morrison, but he told her about his two encounters with Jonesy.

When David reached the part of his story where he discovered that Jonesy had also lost his tongue, Sarah stood up.

"David, stop it, you're scaring me," she snapped.

"Shh, Sarah. I know," David went on, "I'm scared too, but I have to tell you. Please, just listen."

Sarah sat down. David told her about the rooster and the words written on the scarecrow's head. He couldn't remember the words exactly, but he could remember their message. This scarecrow was supposed to scare off anybody who threatened the farm.

"David, this isn't funny. If you're messing with me, I am going to make sure you regret it," Sarah demanded, not knowing whether to believe her brother or not. Certainly Sarah could see that her brother appeared to be seriously upset. But her brother had proved before that he could be as good an actor as anyone.

"Sarah, this is all true, honestly. You have to believe me," pleaded David.

"David, do you realize what you are suggesting? Do you realize what all this will mean if it's true?" Sarah asked nervously. "If this is true, it means our scarecrow is running around scaring and maiming anyone who comes near our farm."

"Only those who threaten it," added David, going over the words in his mind.

"But why the tongues? What's the point of the missing tongues?" Sarah asked.

"I'm not sure," replied David. "Maybe it's to try to stop them from saying what they've seen."

"Maybe," Sarah continued, "but what about the animals, the dog and the rooster? Why harm them?"

David thought for a moment. He tried to remember the words on the scarecrow's head.

"I think the words said something about threatening the farm's peace. Sandy was always barking, especially at night, and that rooster made a lot of noise. Maybe the scarecrow saw them as a threat to the farm's peace. We brought them with us from the old farm. So maybe he thought he had to scare them off too," suggested David.

He really was confused now. But he was more sure than ever that the farm scarecrow had something to do with Morrison, Old Jonesy, his dog, and the dead rooster. The words on the scarecrow's head were the final confirmation.

Sarah moved over to the kitchen window. The image of the scarecrow was growing in her mind. She strained her eyes trying to make out the figure in the field through the evening darkness.

Sarah spoke nervously, "David." Her voice began to tremble. "David, come here. Look."

David joined her at the window and looked out.

"Oh no!" he said under his breath. "Oh, no!"

David ran to the kitchen door and sped across

the yard to the fence. His sister followed but stayed a few feet behind. The two of them stared into the field. The empty field. The scarecrow was gone.

The spot where David had been only ten minutes before was clear except for the small pile of bricks.

"What do we do now, David?" Sarah asked, almost in tears. "I'm really scared."

David stared out into the empty field. He had to tell his dad now. Surely when he saw the empty field he would believe the scarecrow was at the root of all of this.

David took his sister's arm and led her back to the kitchen. As they were entering the kitchen, they could hear someone coming in from the living room.

"Hi, kids, what are you two up to?" Mr. Davies asked, throwing his newspaper into the trash. "The game's starting in a minute, David."

David didn't know where to start. He looked at

Sarah's worried face. He had to tell him.

"Dad," he stammered, "the scarecrow…" He hesitated as he could see the expression on his dad's face change. He knew his dad would take some convincing. But the missing scarecrow now would be the evidence David needed to get his dad to piece all the events together, just as he had done.

"Dad, look at the scarecrow," David continued nervously. Mr. Davies was already standing at the kitchen sink cleaning some dishes.

"Now, David, I don't want to hear any more of this scarecrow business. That guy the other night was just a nutcase," Mr. Davies snapped.

"Dad, please, just look," David cried pleadingly.

"Okay, okay, I'm looking, so what?" replied Mr. Davies.

"Dad, can't you see? The scarecrow is missing," David said, almost pleading with his father to acknowledge what he and his sister had just witnessed.

"David, what are you talking about? It's right there, where it normally is. What's gotten into you today?" Mr. Davies replied, putting the towel in his hand over the chair and heading back to the living room.

David went over to the window and looked out. Sarah joined him. They both looked out again into the darkness toward the field they had been to only a few minutes ago.

The scarecrow was there, standing still in its usual position.

CHAPTER SEVEN

The Banker

David woke up very tired the next morning. He had hardly slept at all that night. After he had seen the scarecrow back in his usual position, David had been unable to tell his dad any more about his theory about what their farm scarecrow was up to. Sarah and he had gone to his room and talked for hours, trying to make some sense of it all. Even after his mom had sent them to bed, Sarah had come back in.

As he climbed out of bed, David wondered for a second if it had all been a dream. He wished it were all a dream. He pulled the window curtain back and looked at the figure in the field.

Who are you and what are you? David thought, the sense of fear beginning to rise in him again. The brief hours of sleep that he had managed to get had been a welcome break from the constant feeling of fear in his head and stomach that had been with him the previous day.

As he headed for the bathroom, Sarah was coming up the stairs. His sister's worried face confirmed that it had been no dream. They were living in a nightmare.

David knew he had to tell his dad. He had decided he would try again that evening. He would write it all down during the day while he was at school, getting it all clear in his own mind, and try to convince him that they had witnessed the scarecrow there one minute, gone the next, only to reappear again. Scarecrows aren't supposed to do that. At least Sarah had been there. She had witnessed the scarecrow's vanishing act.

They had agreed to not mention anything until

they got home from school later. They would then sit their dad down in the living room and explain it all.

David got dressed slowly. As he came down the stairs, he could hear his parents' voices clearly in the kitchen. Sarah and Emma were still in their rooms, so his mom and dad were alone in the kitchen. David hesitated as their voices were becoming louder. They were arguing.

They rarely argued. Mr. Davies usually went out of his way to make sure his wife was happy and she did the same for him. David wondered what the problem was. He silently continued down the stairs and stopped on the bottom step and listened.

"But this is serious this time, John," Mrs. Davies said anxiously. "What are we going to do?"

"Listen, Karen, don't worry. We have had money problems before and we have always come through. We'll figure this one out too," replied Mr. Davies, trying to calm his wife.

"Yes, but how? How do we find the money this time? You said you had been to all the banks, and they couldn't help us. What's left to do? We are going to lose it all," Mrs. Davies continued.

David could sense his mom was now crying.

"Don't be upset, Karen. We'll work it out," replied Mr. Davies. "Mr. Kerr, the manager, is coming over this evening. I am sure he will try to help us. He was the one who agreed to the mortgage on the farm in the first place, so he's bound to want to help."

"But he's the man who wrote this letter. He's the one who is bringing the whole matter to a head. John, you will have to come up with something else," Mrs. Davies insisted, her voice trembling.

"We'll see tonight. I'll know more after I talk to Mr. Kerr. Don't worry, honey. Come on, the children will be down in a minute. Don't let them see that you're upset. We don't want to worry them," said Mr. Davies.

David slowly went back upstairs. He didn't want to see his mom crying.

His sisters were still in their rooms. He could hear Emma singing along to some song she liked, and Sarah was obviously drying her hair, the noise of the hair dryer competing with the music.

David grabbed his backpack, making sure he had everything he needed. He had forgotten, for the time being, about the scarecrow. The conversation downstairs was bothering him now. He knew his dad had borrowed a lot of money to buy the farm. He had explained that to all of them when he warned them that there would be no big vacations for a year or two, at least not until he could get the first couple of harvests in. Something must have happened.

David looked out the window. He caught sight of the scarecrow again. Now we have two big problems, he thought.

The day passed slowly at school. David found

it impossible to concentrate. His teacher had yelled at him a few times for staring into space. David had considered telling his teacher, but he didn't know her well yet. He had wished he had been back at his old school. Mr. Cairns, his old teacher, would have listened to his story about the scarecrow. He would have known what to do.

David had seen Sarah at lunchtime. Her teacher had almost sent her home. Her face was so white, and she had been physically sick that morning. But Sarah wanted to spend as much time away from the farm as she could—away from the scarecrow.

David was relieved when the last bell rang. He had been preparing himself all day. Trying to work out how to tell his dad about the scarecrow. But now there was this money business. It was going to be hard to get his dad's attention.

David sat beside Sarah on the bus home, but they didn't say a word. Emma had gone straight to a friend's house to sleep over. The two of them stepped off the bus and slowly walked up the path to the farmhouse. David couldn't resist looking over to the field. Sarah stared at the ground. She didn't lift her eyes until they entered the house.

"Hi kids, we're going to have an early dinner tonight. Dad's got a visitor coming," Mrs. Davies announced as they entered the kitchen. "Go and do your homework right away. It'll be ready in about forty-five minutes," she added.

David and Sarah went up to their rooms. David decided it would probably be better to talk to his dad after he met the bank manager. If David had understood what this morning's conversation between his parents was about, he was sure that his dad would be in no mood to listen to his son's crazy story. He was sure his dad would sort everything out and would be in a better mood later.

Mr. Davies was in the room that he used as a study (next to the living room), he kept all his paperwork there. There was a lot of paperwork required for running a farm. He sat at his desk, going through the numbers over and over again. He knew he was in real trouble this time. He had borrowed a lot of money to buy the farm, and he had agreed to specific payment terms. He had agreed to pay back large sums of the loan after each harvest. The first big payment was supposed to be due later that year. It was only early spring and harvest time was months away. But for some inexplicable reason, the bank was insisting that the first payment be made now. There was no way that Mr. Davies could come up with the first payment now. He had put all his savings into the farm.

He had tried other banks, but they had not been willing to lend him any money. He had tried to explain that it was only for a few months. But it had been in vain.

Mr. Davies had heard a rumor that there was some property developer interested in building on the land. He had even heard that somebody wanted to build a golf course and country club. Mrs. Tomms, the old woman who had sold him the farm, had mentioned something about it. Apparently, she had been offered a lot of money several times to sell out. But she had wanted the property to remain a farm. Her husband had been a farmer all his life and loved working the land.

He couldn't understand the bank's attitude. Why were they changing the arrangements of the loan? Surely Mr. Kerr would be reasonable. He was relying on it.

They had just finished dinner when Mr. Kerr arrived. David remembered seeing him before when his dad was buying the farm. He had seemed nice enough then. David even remembered him talking to him about baseball.

Mr. Davies and Mr. Kerr disappeared into the living room. Mrs. Davies ran around preparing snacks and coffee. She was obviously anxious.

David hadn't said anything to his sisters about what he had heard his mom and dad talking about. He didn't see any point. Sarah was already upset enough.

The two men seemed to be locked in the room forever! Occasionally, David could hear his dad's voice raised, but he couldn't make out what was being said. It didn't sound as if it was going well. David looked at the alarm clock in his room. Mr. Kerr had been there for almost two hours. Eventually, David heard the living room door open. He ran to the top of the stairs.

"I am sorry, Mr. Davies, that's the way it has to be," David heard the deep voice that he recognized as Mr. Kerr's say.

"We've been over all of this enough. I'm sorry, but I have to go. I've spent too much time on this already. Either get the money to the bank by end of day Monday or lose the farm. That's our decision," Mr. Kerr added sternly.

"But I still don't understand. What caused you to change what we had agreed upon? If this has to do with that golf development, I'll take you all to court," Mr. Davies stated angrily.

"I'm sorry, I have to go. Do what you want, but if we don't see you on Monday, repossession papers will be served first thing Tuesday morning," Mr. Kerr said as he went out the front door.

David heard his dad slam the front door shut.

CHAPTER EIGHT

All Wet

Mr. Kerr rushed from the house, protecting himself from the heavy rain with his briefcase. He jumped into his car, a brand new white BMW. David watched him from his bedroom window. David was reluctant to go anywhere near his dad right now.

In the car, Mr. Kerr struggled to keep his face straight. As soon as he had driven out of the farm gates and onto the main road, a broad grin appeared on his face. He quickly dialed a number on his phone.

After a couple of rings, someone answered.

"It's done. A few more days and we're on our

way. This is the big one, Jim. We'll make a cool million from this deal," Mr. Kerr spoke loudly, battling against the noise of the car.

"How did it go? No problems?" asked Jim Cullen, Mr. Kerr's business associate.

"No problem at all," replied Mr. Kerr. "He is just a small-time farmer. I had to really sell it, of course. Pretend that we tried to help him."

"Does he suspect anything?" Mr. Cullen asked, sounding a little less composed than his partner.

"Well, he has heard about the development. Threatened to take us to court. But he'll never be able to prove anything. I've covered all our tracks," replied Mr. Kerr

"I hope you have. I really hope you have," Mr. Cullen stated nervously.

"Don't worry, Jim. I've taken care of everything. Once we serve the papers on Tuesday, we can celebrate. Until then, business as usual. See you tomorrow. Bye."

Mr. Kerr pressed the end call button on the phone. He looked in the rear-view mirror and allowed himself another smile. You've made it now. You're in the big time, he thought as he looked at himself.

Mr. Kerr had been manager of the local bank for five years. He had worked up from a clerk position to running the bank. He had always been ambitious. To most, Mr. Kerr's career would have been considered a success. Not to Mr. Kerr. He thought he deserved better. He had been really irked when he was passed over twice for a promotion at the bank's headquarters. He hated being stuck in a small rural town pandering, as he saw it, to farmers.

Now he was using his position at the bank to cheat a family out of their home and livelihood just to get what he wanted—money. He had already signed agreements with a major development company. His dream was going to be reality.

He smiled again.

The road ahead was very dark, but the new car's powerful headlights were casting a wide, bright beam. Mr. Kerr lived on the other side of town, but the country roads were quiet, and it wouldn't take him long to cover the few extra miles. As the car approached a sharp bend, Mr. Kerr slowed down. He knew the road well. Just beyond the corner stood the old stone bridge spanning the river. As his car came around the bend, the headlights showed some obstruction blocking the road.

"What now?" exclaimed Mr. Kerr impatiently under his breath. It was now raining very heavily and the last thing he wanted was to get out in the rain and struggle with some fallen tree. He could see now that it was a tree blocking the road. It didn't occur to Mr. Kerr that it was very strange for a tree to end up covering a bridge with water on either side.

Mr. Kerr stopped the car a few yards short of where the tree was and turned the engine off. He stared out of his windshield for a few minutes, shook his head, and then reached for the door handle. As he stepped out of the car, he immediately felt the rain pelting down on him. He cursed the weather and walked up to the tree and stood over it. There was no way, it seemed, that he was going to be able to move it. He put his foot on top of the tree, testing if it could be rolled away. It wouldn't budge.

Suddenly, a loud noise came from behind him. Mr. Kerr immediately recognized the sound as his own car's high-pitched revving.

Someone had gotten into his car, turned the car on, and was revving the engine.

"What on earth! What do you think you are doing?" Mr. Kerr shouted angrily, peering through the headlight's beam. He lifted his hand to his eyes, trying to block the glare and make out who was sitting behind the wheel of his car. The glare was strong and he could see nothing except what looked like a hat.

He started to move toward the car. But as he did, the car started to move toward him.

"Stop right there!" Mr. Kerr shouted, his anger rising.

The car was closing in on him. It started to move more quickly. Mr. Kerr took a couple steps back. He tried again to make out who was on the other side of the windshield. He still couldn't see clearly with the lights blinding him. The car kept coming. His anger quickly turned to fear as he sensed he was in real danger. The fear was paralyzing him.

Mr. Kerr made a move to his left, trying to get out of the car's path. But as he did, the car immediately turned and continued straight for him. Mr. Kerr looked around. The tree was behind him to his right now. Its long branches blocking his way and impeding his retreat. To his left, the bridge wall. He edged backwards. The car kept coming. There was only one way to go. He had to jump onto the wall. The bridge wall was very narrow, only about five inches wide. Mr. Kerr put his hand on top of the wall and hopped up. He wavered slightly, his arms flapping. His upper body leaned over, his eyes fixed on the water below. The heavy rain had turned the normally quiet river into a raging torrent. Mr. Kerr regained his balance and turned around.

"This isn't funny anymore!" he shouted, trying to inject some form of authority into his wavering voice. "Get out of my car!" he screamed.

As if in reply to Mr. Kerr's demand, the car stopped inches from the wall and the car door started to open. Slowly the dark figure got out. Mr. Kerr narrowed his eyes, following the stranger's movements as he came around from behind the car door.

Mr. Kerr stared hard. As the effects of the glare from the headlights disappeared, the figure became clearer.

"Oh my God! What the…?"

The horror in his voice was chilling.

Mr. Kerr moved to step back, forgetting where he was. As he wavered, his feet struggled to retain their grip. It was too late. He couldn't stop himself. He was going over.

As he fell back, he managed to grab the wall with one hand, the skin tearing from his fingers as they tried to hold his full weight. His hand was slipping. He stretched out with the other hand, trying to get another hold on the wall. He couldn't make it.

He looked at the rushing water below. "Help! Help me, please!" Mr. Kerr pleaded.

The pain in his fingers was too strong, the weight too much. He started to slip away. As his hand came away from the wall and he began his fall into the water, he caught a glimpse of a head leaning over the wall. It was a wooden head.

The noise of the wind and the rain drowned out his screams as he plunged into the rushing water.

The scarecrow turned away.

CHAPTER NINE

Do Not Stand in My Way

The next morning, the Davies' house was somber. Everyone could see that Mr. Davies was in a terrible mood. David had heard his mother crying for most of the night. Even now her eyes were red and sore. David's were too. He had managed to sleep very little over the past two nights, and he still hadn't been able to talk to his dad. Mr. Davies had stormed out minutes after Mr. Kerr had left and hadn't returned until after everyone had gone to bed.

Sarah and Emma had no idea what was going on, but David knew the family was in serious trouble. He had heard Mr. Kerr's ultimatum.

His dad had to pay the bank by Monday or they were going to lose the farm.

David was glad it was Saturday. He couldn't have faced school again. He was a mess. He was tired, confused, worried, and scared.

His dad was messing around in the barn, repairing the digger. It had suddenly broken down first thing that morning as he had started to clear the field in front—the field with the scarecrow in it.

David was waiting for his dad to come in. He had made up his mind that no matter what, he had to tell his dad about the scarecrow. Even if his dad refused to accept what he was saying, at least he would get it off his chest. He felt so lonely and isolated. There was, of course, Sarah, but he needed his dad to know.

As David waited, the phone rang. Sarah ran to answer it, expecting to hear her friend's voice. She was expecting a call, but when she answered, she was disappointed.

"Mom, it's Officer Collins again," she shouted, trying to reach her mom upstairs.

Mrs. Davies came down, the Morrison incident long replaced by the worries of the family's financial problems.

She took the receiver from Emma.

"Hello officer, how can I help you?" she asked.

David moved into the hallway where his mother was taking the call. He watched as the shock appeared on her face. She put her hand over the receiver.

"David, go and get your dad, quickly!" she ordered.

David could see the anxiety in her eyes and spun around immediately running to get his dad.

The two returned quickly. Mrs. Davies was standing by the telephone. She was rooted to the spot since Officer Collins had hung up.

Mr. Davies rushed to his wife's side, anticipating that her legs were about to give out on her.

He ushered her into the living room.

Mrs. Davies spoke first. "He was sitting on that chair only a few hours ago."

"What is it? What happened now?" asked Mr. Davies, confused and worried.

Mrs. Davies relayed her brief conversation with Officer Collins. She explained that they had found Mr. Kerr's car in the river this morning.

"He is missing but they are out searching for him. The river was so high last night, he must have been swept up in it. They are looking downstream for him now. "

"But, how on earth? Where did this happen?" interrupted Mr. Davies.

"Next to the old bridge, on the way to town. They can't understand what happened to him. They couldn't find evidence of the car losing control on the road. It looks like he just calmly drove up and into the river," Mrs. Davies replied, her eyes filling up.

"Oh, John! What's going on? First that man the other night and now this. What's going on?" Mrs. Davies pleaded, beginning to break down.

Mr. Davies held his wife in his arms, trying to comfort her. His mind drifted to the meeting he had held with Mr. Kerr the night before.

David had listened to his mom relaying the news about Mr. Kerr. It didn't take him long to add the Mr. Kerr incident to all the others. Mr. Kerr was threatening the farm. David had also heard the rumors about the golf course development. Most of the town seemed to know that Mr. Kerr had wanted their farm for some time. Last night it had looked as if he was about to get his way with the Monday deadline.

David didn't buy the police officer's story. Something or somebody was to blame. David knew it had to be the scarecrow.

David waited for his dad to come out of the living room.

"Dad, I have to talk to you," David started.

"Is it important, son? I need to see to your mom. She is really upset," replied Mr. Davies.

"Dad, before I tell you anything, I need you to come outside with me. I need you to look at the scarecrow with me," David continued.

"Look, son, enough of this nonsense," Mr. Davies snapped.

"Dad, just do it, okay!" David insisted, raising his voice.

Mr. Davies was taken aback by his son's tone. He recognized that there was something upsetting David. He put his arm around him.

"Come on, let's go," Mr. Davies said, heading for the kitchen door.

The two crossed the yard in silence, climbed the fence, and made their way across the field to where the scarecrow stood. David approached the wooden figure nervously. Mr. Davies could see that his son was really bothered by the scarecrow.

David lifted the hat from the scarecrow's head and pointed to the words engraved on top.

Mr. Davies was a good eighteen inches taller than his son and could easily see the words written on the bald head.

This land is yours for you to scare

All beings who perchance do dare

To disturb or threaten without pity

This house's peace and prosperity.

The big farmer looked at his son and then read the words again, as if to make sure he understood their meaning.

"I have no idea what to think," he said, shaking his head. "Let's go back."

They walked slowly back toward the house. On the way, David rapidly ran through all the events of the past few days, connecting everything back to the eerie words written on the scarecrow's head. In every case, the person or animal affected had been connected to the farm and in some way threatening or disturbing it.

David told his dad about witnessing the scarecrow disappearing and then reappearing.

When they reached the kitchen door, Mr. Davies looked back. The scarecrow looked so normal, like all the scarecrows he had seen in all the years he had been working as a farmer.

As they entered the kitchen, Mr. Davies took his son's arm.

"Listen, son. Don't say a word of this to anyone. Especially not to your mother. She is at her wits' end at the moment. I'll have to think about this for a while. I don't want to make us the laughingstock of the whole town." He paused, his mind struggling to accept what seemed inconceivable.

But he was beginning to share his son's anxiousness. At least, he thought, if there was something going on, it didn't seem to be posing any threat to his family. If it was the scarecrow, it seemed to be trying to protect them.

"I have to go into town and go to the bank to see how things stand for Monday," said Mr. Davies. "I don't know how this business with Mr. Kerr is going to affect things. When I come back, we'll light a fire and burn the thing, and then let's see what happens."

Mr. Davies left ten minutes later. The bank was usually closed on Saturdays, but Mr. Davies had managed to get someone on the phone. As the news had broken about their manager, some of the staff had gone in to find out more.

David was worried. He had felt better telling his dad and he was happy to see that his dad seemed to share his concerns; however, he wished that they had dealt with the scarecrow before he had left for town.

The hours passed slowly. David remained in his

room until late afternoon. His dad had still not come back. He tried to keep his mind off things by playing his guitar and some video games. But his mind kept wandering to the scarecrow. Eventually he pulled back his curtains to look at the wooden man.

David stepped back. The fear returned in a flash. The scarecrow was gone. He ran downstairs and scanned the yard from the kitchen door.

Did Dad come back and take the horrible thing away to burn it, he thought more in hope than anything.

He ran out to see if he could see his dad's car or his dad himself. There was no sign.

He heard a noise from the barn. He hesitated and then walked toward the entrance. Suddenly, from inside, he heard a voice.

"Looking for me, David?"

David froze. It was not his dad's voice. It was not any voice he recognized. He could sense the presence in the barn before he could see it. He entered the barn, his legs like jelly, the fear taking over his body.

"Hello, David."

The wooden scarecrow stepped from behind some bales of hay, moving in a slow, deliberate manner.

David stood motionless, unable to speak. All his fears were now a reality. Morrison had not been a madman. As far as he could tell, this "thing" in front of him was really dangerous.

The scarecrow's strained, slightly high-pitched voice continued. "David, do not stand in my way. I was made for this. I am doing what I must do."

David struggled to speak, his throat and lips completely dry. Eventually he blurted out, "But why?"

"I serve the farm, David. I was made to protect it. People are not important. People come and go, but the land remains forever. I serve the land. The farm and the land," the scarecrow replied.

The significance of the scarecrow's words hit David. The scarecrow wasn't protecting them, it was only interested in the farm and the land. Anything that threatened the land was in danger.

"Do not stand in my way, David. Do not try to stop me. Heed my words," the scarecrow hissed.

He moved toward David. David closed his eyes, paralyzed by fear. He felt the scarecrow brush past him. His legs wavered. He felt the scarecrow's presence disappear. David opened his eyes. He was alone. He fell to the floor, his legs finally giving out.

CHAPTER TEN

Fire

"David! David!"

David opened his eyes. Sarah was standing above him.

"What happened to you, David? Are you okay?" Sarah asked, a little shocked by the sight of her brother sprawled on the barn floor.

David picked himself up, his legs still a little unsteady and his head sore from hitting the barn floor. He had been unconscious for an hour or so. He immediately looked beyond his sister. In the field behind her, he could see the still, dark figure back in its usual spot.

"Come on, Sarah. Let's get out of here," David

stated, grabbing his sister's arm. "Now!" he insisted as his sister hesitated, staring out into the field and sensing the scarecrow was the reason for her brother's state.

They ran back to the kitchen. Mrs. Davies was working at the sink. David and Sarah walked through the kitchen and went upstairs.

"What is it, David? What is going on?" Sarah asked anxiously.

"We are in danger, Sarah. Real danger," David replied.

David told her about his encounter in the barn. Sarah buried her head in her pillow, her brother's words sending a chill right through her.

"Sarah, I want you to get Mom and take her into the living room and keep her there. Make up some story about school. Keep her talking. Don't come out until I get back."

"David, where are you going? What are you going to do?" Sarah pleaded, unsure what was going through her brother's mind.

David knew what he had to do. He couldn't afford to wait until his dad got home. He was going to have to do it himself. His family was in danger, and he had no idea when the scarecrow was going to strike again or against whom. He was already getting worried that his dad had taken so long. Maybe the scarecrow would see his family as a threat. Maybe it would blame them if the farm were ripped up and turned into a golf course.

"Go Sarah, get Mom!" David said, pacing the room, thinking his way through his next move.

David heard his mom and Sarah go into the living room. He ran downstairs, out the kitchen door, and into the shed. He knew what he was looking for. He had seen it there the other day. Where was it now? David moved his bike. There it was.

David picked up the old oil lamp. He lifted the lid. Good, there was plenty of oil in the bottom.

David ran back to the kitchen. It was getting dark now. David searched in the sink drawer. He found the box of matches and stuffed them into his pocket.

He ran to the barn and grabbed as much hay as he could carry. He stopped as he came out of the barn and looked into the field. The scarecrow was still. David took a few deep breaths and walked forward. He climbed the fence, careful not to spill the oil from the lamp. As he approached the wooden monster, he had no idea what to expect. He kept his eyes fixed on it. It could move at any point. He had to take his chance. He had no idea what governed when and how the scarecrow could come to life. He had to protect his family.

David came up to the scarecrow and started wrapping the hay around the monster's legs. David didn't take his eyes off the scarecrow's face—no movement, thank God. He searched in his pocket. The matches weren't there. His blood rushed.

Other pocket! He found them. He had to put the lamp down to light the match. The match lit first try. He put it to the wick.

"Come on, come on," he pleaded, urging the wick to light. The wick flickered and the flame took hold. He lifted the lamp above his head, preparing himself to smash it down with all his force at the base of the scarecrow. He hesitated. He could hear the sound of a car approaching.

David glanced around, hoping to see his dad's car. As he turned away, his eyes momentarily leaving the monster's face, he felt something grab the lamp. He spun around, and the scarecrow's face was smiling an evil smile. The scarecrow reached out, its hand tightening around David's neck. David lashed out and ran. He could hear the scarecrow following behind, its legs speeding through the overgrown grass. He could sense he was close.

David clambered over the fence, as he had done

the previous day when he had read the words on the scarecrow's head. As he landed on the other side, the scarecrow landed too. The monster still held the oil lamp. The lamp's glow cast an eerie light across the scarecrow's face. The scarecrow moved around, blocking David's path to the house.

David looked around, his desire for survival controlling his fear. He started to go right, stopped, and darted left toward the barn.

He ran in and buried himself behind some bales of hay, the chickens flapping nervously at the noise of him rushing in. The scarecrow followed slowly, knowing he had his prey trapped.

David could see the light from the lamp's glow lighting up the entrance as the scarecrow walked in. He crouched down, trying to calm his breathing, trying to think what to do next. He lifted his head slightly. His eyes found a gap between two bales. Peering through the bales, he could trace the scarecrow's movements by the movements of the light. He was coming closer.

The scarecrow's chilling voice broke the silence.

"David, I warned you. Now you must pay the price."

David looked up. The bales of hay were piled three high. The scarecrow was directly in front of him now, on the other side of the bales.

David took a couple of steps back and steadied himself. The scarecrow spun around, sensing David's movement. David ran, jumped, and launched himself at the bales of hay. The stack wavered.

The scarecrow looked up just as the first bale hit him. The oil lamp smashed to the floor and burst into flames. The scarecrow's legs and arms, stuffed with hay, immediately caught fire. Within seconds, the bales all over the barn were in flames. The chickens scampered frantically trying to make their exit, their noise adding to the chaotic scene.

David tried to pick himself off the floor, but

the whole barn now seemed like one big ball of fire. He could just make out the spot where the scarecrow had been. He caught sight of something. He recognized the scarecrow's old hat. He couldn't see anything else except flames. He started to crawl forward, the smoke beginning to enter his lungs. His head started to sway. He started to cough, struggling for every breath. The heat was overpowering.

Suddenly, he felt something reaching for him, pulling at his legs. He tried to kick free, crawl away, but the smoke had taken its toll and he had no strength. He could run no more. He felt himself being lifted in the air. His heart was pounding. He was helpless.

"Come on, son. Let's get you out of here." Mr. Davies threw his son over his shoulder and rushed out of the barn.

He placed his son against the kitchen door. David struggled to catch his breath, the smoke still deep inside his lungs. He felt his mom's arms around him, his head still swimming and his vision blurred. Mrs. Davies hugged him tightly, shocked at the sight of her son.

Mr. Davies knelt down in front of his son.

"Is it all over, Davey? Is he gone?" Mr. Davies asked, two hands on his son's shoulders.

David looked at the barn, the flames leaping high into the sky. He looked back at his dad and nodded his head.

"He's gone, Dad."

David stood up and took a few steps toward the barn. Mr. Davies came and stood by his side. They stared at the wall of flames in front of them.

"The farm is safe, son. We're going to be fine," Mr. Davies said, his broad arm over his son's shoulder.

"The scarecrow saw to it all, Dad. I am sure of it," David said, looking up at his father. "He wasn't interested in anything else, only the farm."

"Well, he has protected it for the last time. It's up to us now," Mr. Davies stated, reassuringly, turning back to the house. "Come on, son. Let's get you inside."

David looked out to the empty field, one last time. At last he felt safe.

EPILOGUE

"David, will you stop reading that paper and give me a hand?" David's wife, Anne, snapped impatiently. "It was your idea to go on a picnic, so come on."

David put down the paper and helped his wife lay out the blanket on the grass. It was Sunday afternoon, and it was a scorcher. As soon as David had woken up that morning and seen the blue sky, he had decided that it was a good day to pack the family in the car and travel to one of their favorite spots in the hills near their home. The kids loved to get out in the open and explore.

The journey had taken them about an hour,

and the two boys, Alan and Paul, had behaved the whole way. Alan had just turned five, and Paul was almost three years old. They were very close and loved to play together.

Within minutes, Anne had covered the blanket with juice and cake for the boys and sandwiches and a bottle of wine for herself and David.

"Go and find the boys, dear, it's ready," Anne said, spotting her husband picking up the paper again.

The boys never wandered far. They were explorers, indeed, but they weren't that brave yet.

David had kept one eye on his sons and seen them wander down a small path a few yards away. David followed the path for about ten to fifteen yards through the trees. He soon heard the noise of the two boys playing. He spotted them halfway up a wooden fence, pointing into the field straight ahead.

The scarecrow stood about twenty yards from

the fence.

The boys heard their dad approach. They turned around to look at him, broad smiles lighting up their faces.

"What are scarecrows supposed to scare, Dad?" Alan asked, looking back at the scarecrow.

"Oh, they look after the crops. They just scare away anything that tries to eat the crops."

"So they're not supposed to scare us?" little Paul asked, innocently.

David smiled, the memories buried deep inside him.

"No, son, they are not supposed to scare us. Come on, let's go. Your mom has some treats for you," he replied, lifting the two boys off the fence, one in each arm. He set them down and started to chase them up the path toward their afternoon picnic.

As the boys ran on, David stopped. He couldn't resist a glance back. His body froze.

The field was empty.

Read on to enjoy an excerpt from another
haunting title in the Creepers series:

Stage Fright

by Edgar J. Hyde

Illustrations by Chloe Tyler

CHAPTER ONE

I'll Take That

The witch's gnarled and twisted hands grasped the stick firmly and stirred the contents of the cauldron. She was the eldest and also the most ugly of the three. Her huge hooked nose stopped just short of touching her top lip and when she spoke you could see that the few remaining teeth she had were blackened and broken with age. She had lost an eye years before in a battle with a winter witch, but rather than wear an eye patch, she simply left the empty socket exposed, black and gruesome.

She began to mumble as she continued stirring, "The freshly cut tail of a gerbil, the liver of a brand new puppy, the heart of a newborn lamb."

She cackled and looked at her two sisters. "So far, so good," she said as her mouth twisted into what was more of an ugly grimace than a smile. "Fetch me the spell book, one of you. Quickly, so that I can see what other ingredients we need."

The witch nearest her went to fetch the book, her huge black dress rustling as she did. Like the others, she was dressed entirely in black from the top of her pointed hat to the tip of her large feet which were clad in huge, black buckled shoes. As with most witches, she had an abundance of warts scattered all over her face, the largest of which hung from the tip of her nose. Unlike her other sisters, though, her eyes were not small and beady. They were a piercing silver and they glinted dangerously as she looked around for the misplaced spell book.

"Over there," said the third sister, pointing as she spoke. But it was not a finger she pointed with, for this sister also had fought a hard battle with the same winter witch years ago and lost, forfeiting her right hand and part of her arm in the process. Her hand and arm were now made of strong metal and though at first the witch had felt disadvantaged, she was now able to accomplish most tasks better than ever before.

She had been able to slit the young pup's tummy, for example, without even having to use a knife, and acquiring the gerbil's tail had been easy and quite enjoyable.

She watched as her sister's eyes shone silver in the darkness as she bent to lift the spell book and bring it back to the fire over which the cauldron bubbled. Just then, there was a huge clap of thunder as the sky grew even darker than before. Lightning forked across the sky and the three witches cackled together at the thought of the impending storm.

"A perfect night, sisters," said the first sister, her stagnant breath mixing with the night air as she spoke. She stopped turning the pages when she reached the spell they were looking for. She ran her blackened fingernail down the page until she found the next ingredient she must put into the cauldron.

"Aha!" She grinned maliciously. "This is one I'm going to enjoy. A young boy's freshly severed finger." She looked at her two sisters and they grinned back. "Bring him to me," she growled.

The two sisters looked delightedly at one another and left the orange glow of the flames, heading toward the bushes that encircled the clearing where they had built their fire. The boy whimpered as they approached. His wrists were raw and bleeding from his struggle to free himself from the thick ropes the witches had used to bind his arms and legs together. His blond hair hung limply on his forehead and tearstains marked his face. He had tried to be brave, after all, thirteen-year-old boys don't cry, but he simply couldn't help it. He was really afraid.

The one with the silver eyes was staring at him, her eyes seeming to burn right through him, as though seeing into his very soul. The other one bent down and released his feet from the ropes with one quick snip from her metal hand. He shivered involuntarily.

"Stand up, boy," she ordered, dragging him toward her as she spoke. The boy winced, partly from the pain of her grasp and also at the sharpness of the odor emanating from both witches.

If I live to be one hundred, he thought, I shall never forget that smell...that is if I live at all.

He was forced to walk toward the cauldron, while thunder clapped and bolts of lightning shot across the sky. As he drew closer to the fire, he could see that the eldest witch was bending down to unwrap something. She unraveled a large piece of black cloth, uncovering a vast selection of shiny steel knives.

The boy drew in his breath sharply. He started to shake almost uncontrollably.

The witch seemed unable to make up her mind about which knife would be best to use and was debating intently over two in particular.

When he was close enough, his two captors pushed him to his knees and began to untie his hands. The witch still looked at the knives.

"If I may make a suggestion, sister," began one, "if you're having difficulty choosing, I could sever the finger now."

She clicked her metal fingers in the air, and the boy began to cry openly.

"Shut up, sniveling little coward," said the witch, deciding eventually on a knife and lifting it into the air with a flourish. She had placed a large rock on the ground and now indicated to her sisters that they should position the boy's hand on top.

He was sobbing now and pleading with them.

"Please," he begged. "Please let me go! Please don't hurt me!"

Annoyed at the boy's struggles and pleas, the witch lifted the knife high into the air.

"Ready?" she asked her two sisters, who

restrained the boy on either side.

They both nodded. As the knife drew closer to his hand, the child screamed and tried in vain to pull away. The cold steel glinted as it made contact and his finger cleanly and neatly severed from his hand, fell noiselessly onto the grass. Blood spurted from the gaping wound, and the witches left the boy to fall down in agony as they watched their sister excitedly lift the severed finger and throw it into the cauldron. Another bolt of thunder followed and they clapped their hands in glee and danced hysterically around the fire.

Two young girls dressed in matching leotards and tap dance shoes walked in front of the steaming cauldron and held up a large sign. Just before the curtain fell, the audience was able to read the sign.

END OF ACT ONE.

CHAPTER TWO

The Wart

Their black costumes, hats, and shoes discarded now in favor of their school uniforms, the three girls sat together in the school cafeteria discussing the rehearsal.

"Don't know if these plastic warts were a good idea," moaned Melissa as she looked in her mirror. "This one on my chin's really stuck. Where on earth did you get them?" she asked Jo.

"From the joke shop in town," replied her friend. "The same place I got the severed finger—wasn't it great?"

"Not as great as these donuts," said Danny Cottrill as he swiped one of their donuts.

"Hey!" cried Jenny, jumping to her feet. "Give that back!"

Danny stopped and turned to face the girls. "Why? What happens if I don't?" He smirked. "Will you cast a spell on me?" And he stuffed half of the stolen donut into his mouth.

"Yeah," shouted Jenny. "You watch yourself, Danny Cottrill, or I'll get my spell book and turn you into a fat, ugly toad. Whoops," she giggled, "I almost forgot—you already are a fat, ugly toad." And she sat back down beside her two friends.

Danny had been too busy laughing at his own joke to hear the last part of what Jenny had to say and made his way through the busy cafeteria, slapping people (who didn't want to be slapped) hard on the back of the head, tripping smaller kids carrying trays of food, and stealing anything within reach.

"Bully," mumbled Melissa, returning her gaze to the mirror and making renewed efforts to remove the offending wart.

"Oh, I wish this thing would just come off," she groaned in exasperation, just as the piece of plastic loosened its grip from her chin and fell onto the table in front of her.

"There ya go!" Jo smiled. "And I didn't even see you cast a spell!"

Melissa smiled back at her friend. "Didn't you hear me utter the magic words: Hocus Pocus. You can wish for anything your heart desires you know, acne-free skin, a spot on the soccer team, a date with Jonathan..."

The three girls sighed as one.

"If only," Melissa sighed. "The day one of us manages to get a date with Jonathan will be nothing short of a miracle."

Jo rubbed at her fingernails. The black nail polish she had just removed had left little flecks on her cuticles.

"Great rehearsal though, girls. Don't you think?

I'm so glad Miss Dobson found the play. It's so dramatic. You could almost hear the sixth graders hold their breath this morning when we rehearsed act one."

Jenny agreed, "Yeah, but I have to admit it's a relief taking the fake arm off after rehearsal. It's hard to maneuver the fingers."

"We could change it, I guess," said Melissa. "I mean, it's not like a mechanical arm was in the original play. Miss Dobson just thought it made *Oh Spirits Obey Us* more updated."

"No, she's right," said Jenny, flexing her hand and fingers. "We should leave it in. It does make the play a little more modern. But wasn't Jonathan great this morning," she sighed longingly. "Those screams were really bloodcurdling, I almost believed him. Anyway, where did you say Miss Dobson got the script from?" She turned to Melissa.

"Apparently," said her friend, "she was cleaning out an old drawer in the drama room a few weeks ago when she came across it. She read it over and liked it instantly, and when she looked in old school records she realized that although it was actually written by a former student, it had never been performed. According to what she was told, all previous attempts to stage the play had ended in failure since the students playing the parts of the witches' enemies had to leave school due to mysterious illnesses. Weird, don't you think?"

"Definitely and just a teensy bit scary," agreed Jo.

"Oh, don't be silly," said Jenny. "You're getting carried away with all this talk of puppies' livers and lambs' hearts. It's just a story."

Just then, the bell rang, signaling the end of lunch. Jenny scrambled on the floor, grabbing the books that had fallen out of her bag and stuffing them back in.

"Gotta go!" she called over her shoulder, after quickly finishing her juice. "I have history next. See you at 3 o'clock."

Jo and Melissa waved goodbye to their friend and made their way to the opposite end of the school.

"Math—ugh!" groaned Melissa, as the two entered the classroom.

"Yeah," whispered Jo, "but at least the view is nice."

Both girls laid their chins on their hands and gazed dreamily at Jonathan for the rest of class.

Be sure to check out the othe

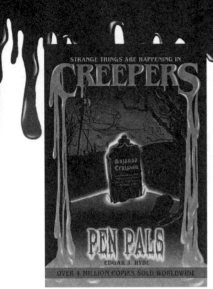

Pen Pals
ISBN: 9781486718757

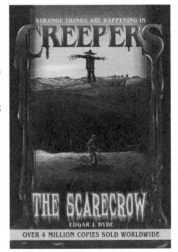

The Scarecrow
ISBN: 9781486718788

Stage Fright
ISBN: 9781486718771

tles in the Creepers series!

The Piano
ISBN: 9781486718764

Cold Kisser
ISBN: 9781486718740

The Gravedigger
ISBN: 9781486718795

Edgar J. Hyde has a message just for you.
If you solve his riddles, prepare for some creepy fun,
and you might even find a surprise waiting for you...
Solve the riddles below and in The Piano, unscramble
the letters, and fill in the blanks of this web URL

www.flowerpotpress.com/_ _ _ _ _ _ _

with the answers you find. Go to the website
with your parent's permission and find out
what waits on the other side.

1. The beginning of this brooding tale is one of fear, contempt, and rage.
An unknown man is found in a barn with no way to explain why he is there.
He is eventually taken by the police. What is the first letter of this man's last name?

2. If you dare disturb this scarecrow's land, you will be met with a terrible fate.
If you wish to not disturb this seemingly inanimate creature, you must heed the writing on
his forehead. What was the final letter of the first line on this scarecrow's head?

3. Mr. Kerr, a vile businessman, was the subject of the scarecrow's ire.
On a bridge with a fallen tree is where we last saw Mr. Kerr conspire.
What letter did Mr. Kerr's very last word begin with before he fell into the river?